CHOOSE YOUR OWN ADVENTURE®

Kids Love Reading
Choose Your Own Adventure®!

"This book was wonderful and cool."
Azailea Morales, age 8

"This book was cool. I thought I would be scared
of the monsters but I really liked them."
Bella Foster, age 6

"This book was awesome. I loved it. It was not too
scary. Homer is so awesome. I love Homer."
Brooke Downing, age 7

"This book was good. I like that I got to
pick how the story went."
Lily Von Trapp, age 7

"The book was funny, whoa!"
Anna Kenyon, age 7

Illustrated by: Keith Newton
Book design: Stacey Boyd, Big Eyedea Visual Design
For information regarding permission, write to:

CHOOSECO
P.O. Box 46
Waitsfield, Vermont 05673
www.cyoa.com

A DRAGONLARK BOOK

ISBN: 1-933390-40-9
EAN: 978-1-933390-40-6

Published simultaneously in the United States and Canada

Printed in China.

1 0 9 8 7 6 5 4 3 2

CHOOSE YOUR OWN ADVENTURE®

RETURN TO HAUNTED HOUSE

BY R. A. MONTGOMERY

A DRAGONLARK BOOK

READ THIS FIRST!!!

WATCH OUT!
THIS BOOK IS DIFFERENT
than *every book you've ever read.*

Do not read this book from the first page through to the last page.
Instead, start on page 1 and read until you come to your first choice. Then turn to the page shown and see what happens.

When you come to the end of a story, you can go back and start again.
Every choice leads to a new adventure.

Good luck!

"Rise and shine, buddy!"

You look up from your pillow. It's Homer, your dog and best friend. He is wearing a goofy cowboy hat left over from Halloween.

"Saddle up. We're hitting the trail," Homer says. Homer talks to you in normal English, but only you understand. To everyone else it's just barks and woofs.

You can barely recognize his voice. He sounds like a Hollywood cowboy. You might as well humor him until he gets over this silliness.

"We're already late!" he adds.

Turn to page 2.

"Late for what?" you ask. A coiled metal spring falls from the ceiling and bounces against your bedspread. Your eyes pop open wide. You are not at home in your bedroom! You are in a strange purple room, with portholes and gears. Your desk and computer still sit next to your bed.

"I received our new assignment. The next great mystery! Our super-excellent adventure. We're on our way to explore the next haunted house!"

Turn to page 4.

4

Homer prances around like popcorn in a hot pan.

"What 'next' haunted house?" you ask. Homer seems to be taking charge.

"We, mainly me, found out about...uh, I mean ...have been invited by...the Interplanetary Society For Haunted...Things..." Homer scratches his side with his left leg. "To investigate," he finishes.

"Great. Where is it?" you ask, intrigued.

"Well, there are two. We get to choose."

Turn to page 6.

"We?" you say. You don't like Homer being so bossy.

"There is an old mansion in England with 60 bedrooms. It has a great hall with a fireplace as wide as a car. The house sits on hundreds of acres of land and forests. It's been cursed, so no one lives there. It's called Montagoo Hall." He pauses. You nod. Sounds like a perfect scary house.

"The other?" you ask.

"The other is a palace in the jungle of Thailand. It was once the home of a Thai king from the Rama dynasty. People say it is haunted by elephant ghosts that keep people from living there or using it. Big danger."

If you choose to investigate Montagoo Hall, turn to page 7.

If you choose to go to Thailand and the ancient Rama palace, turn to page 14.

"I knew you'd choose Montagoo Hall. I just knew it," says Homer. He gives you a funny little smile and wags his tail. His whiskers curl and shake.

"What does that mean?" you reply. "I think it sounds like an interesting place."

"Mmm-hmm yes, completely agree," Homer answers mysteriously. He pretends to make some notes in a notebook just like the one you use when you're working as a detective.

"Homer, what is this contraption we're in?"

"It's a Socko Skidder—it's a cross between a time machine and an airplane. I bought it at the junkyard. I fixed it up a little. HOLD ON!!!" he yells.

Turn to page 8.

The Socko Skidder zooms through time and space and lands with a huge squishy thud in a field overgrown with grass and flowers. A dark forest surrounds the field on three sides.

On the fourth side stands a big old brick mansion. The building stretches for hundreds of yards, bursting with chimneys and turrets. It has hundreds of glass windows, but some are broken.

Smoke curls into the sky from one small chimney at the back of the mansion.

This is Montagoo Hall.

Turn to page 10.

You walk up to the front door of the house. The door is heavy-looking and made of wood. It slowly swings open. You look at Homer.

"Creepy!" you say. Homer's tail is between his legs and he does not answer. You both step inside. You feel evil in this house.

The door closes with a loud bang. You and Homer are left alone in the Great Hall. It is cold, with stone floors and stone walls, like the entrance to a castle.

You imagine the people who lived here in the past. Earls, or barons—and their servants,

cooks, maids and butlers. Who built this mansion, you wonder? Who is responsible for the haunting of Montagoo Hall?

Turn to page 12.

"Come in, come in," says a creaky voice. "Don't be afraid."

Who is that? You look at Homer. He is cowering behind you with his front paws over his ears. His cowboy hat is gone. You look up, where small hawks have settled in the rafters. They look at each other, at the ceiling, down the hall—anywhere but you. They don't know what's going on.

"Come in, Come in!"

If you overcome your fear and enter, turn to page 20.

If you decide to leave this scary place now, turn to page 24.

You look at Homer. What a great dog, you think. He is your closest friend. Plus he knows a lot! He is like a walking Google search.

"So, Homer, here we are in the Socko Skidder heading to Thailand and some lost palace. What do you know?"

"What do you want to know?" he replies. "Thailand used to be called *Siam*, but that changed hundreds of years ago. It is a wonderful country. The Mekong River runs through it, so does the Chao Phraya. The Rama kings have been around since 1782!"

"Kings?" you ask. "Are there kings today?"

INDIAN OCEAN

Turn to page 17.

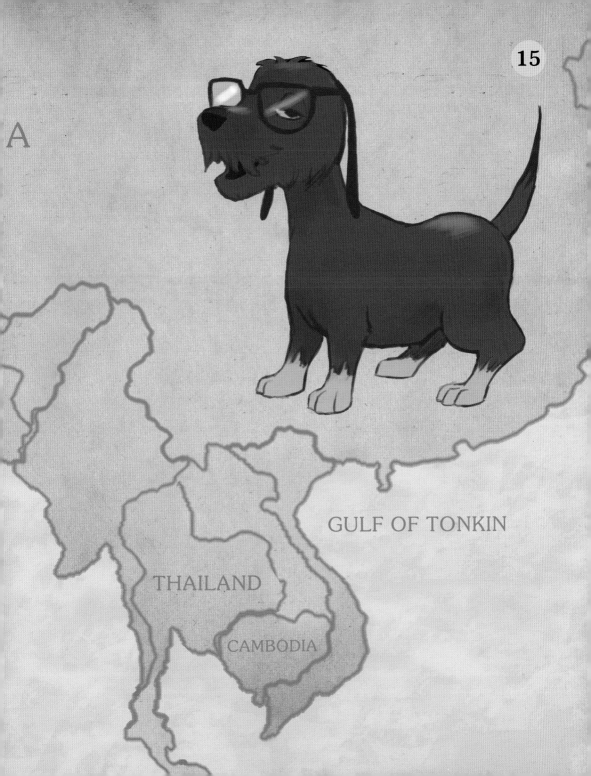

A

GULF OF TONKIN

THAILAND

CAMBODIA

"The current king is Rama IX or King Bhumibol. He does not actually rule. But the people love him and follow his advice." Homer scratches a flea and yawns. It's been a long day.

Bump! Splotch! Zonk! Your Socko Skidder transport comes to rest in a jungle clearing. There is no pilot. It is programmed to take you where you want to go. Time to get out. It's time to find the hidden, forgotten palaces and temples of the early Rama kings.

The jungle is thick and smells of rare flowers.

Turn to page 18.

"Yieee!" come the screeches from a cluster of monkeys. They swing from trees and rush into the jungle, right past you.

Next you hear what sounds like bulldozers, with trumpets!

It must be elephants!

Elephants were the old battle-wagons of ancient Siam. They are ferocious fighters. They are rumored to protect the old temple and palace you are visiting. You need to run for it! But where to?

Turn to page 26.

20

You and Homer walk through the hallway and enter a bright, open room with many chairs and a broken grand piano.

At the edge of the room, by a large stained-glass window, you spy a light. It sparkles, grows brighter, and then changes colors. It goes from yellow to purple and red. You are drawn closer and closer. Music slips along the walls and swirls around you. It is flute music and drum music. You like it.

Turn to page 23.

"*Alea iacta est!*" Latin words boom from the direction of the glowing light.

"What?" you ask.

"It's Latin!" says Homer. "It means 'the die is cast.' You can't turn back. Too late to change our minds. Julius Caesar said it when he reached a river called the Rubicon. It meant that he was committed to war." Homer stands right by your side. "I think it's a warning."

Turn to page 50.

24

"Let's 23 skiddoo, pardner," Homer woofs. He's already headed for the door.

"What are you talking about, Homer?" you ask. "23 skiddoo?"

Homer lopes outside. "It's slang for *let's scram!*"

Whammo! Zingo! Homer falls flat on his face, bending his whiskers.

"Not so fast, my furry friend," says a scratchy voice from inside the huge mansion. "We have plans for you!"

There is a terrible screeching sound, like an old tin can is being ripped apart by kindergarten scissors.

You don't like the sound of "plans." You don't like Montagoo Hall or the creaky old voice that stopped Homer in his tracks. You want OUT and NOW!!

"You are too slow! Now I must have you escorted in." The baby hawks soar by as the creaky voice trails off.

Go on to the next page.

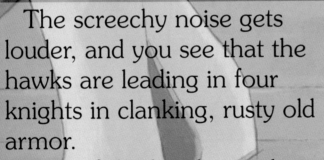

The screechy noise gets louder, and you see that the hawks are leading in four knights in clanking, rusty old armor.

Two of the knights grab you and Homer, and two more throw a finely woven net on you. Yuck! It's a spiderweb.

Turn to page 39.

Out of nowhere, a small child appears and tugs at your hand. His skin is golden brown and he wears a torn white shirt and black shorts. He is barefoot.

"Follow me," he says in English. "I'll get you to safety. The elephants are angry."

Homer eyes the small boy and says, "I don't know. I think we're better off on our own."

"What's your name?" you ask the boy.

"Pong," he replies. "And I have a brother named Ding and a sister named Song. You'll like them. We live in the palace."

If you decide to follow the boy, turn to page 28.

If you decide that Homer is right, then say thanks to Pong and go off on your own. Who knows who Pong really is? He could be pretending to be friendly. Maybe he is a spirit or a ghost. Turn to page 34.

Homer is often right, but your instinct says that you can trust Pong.

"Let's follow Pong," you say.

You reach for Pong's hand. He clasps it and leads you and Homer on a path into the jungle.

Go on to the next page.

Suddenly, six large elephants break through the tree line. Their trunks are high, and their ears are flared. They make sharp screeches like sirens coming. They smash trees and stamp the ground.

"Follow me! Come quick!" Pong yells.

Turn to page 30.

Pong veers off, away from the elephants. The jungle mysteriously opens for him. Homer runs behind you. You can feel his hot breath on your legs.

In a clearing, you see a huge palace over-grown with vines and flowers and trees and bushes. A golden spire shoots up to the sky. Birds of all sorts–parrots, doves, and cranes–zoom upwards like a halo over the palace.

"Come in," Pong says. "It is safe here." Two children stand next to a huge pillar. They smile at you and wave.

Just then a scream shoots through the soft, golden light. It is the scream of someone or something in great agony.

"Not to worry," Pong says. "That's a monkey scream. Scary, isn't it?"

Turn to page 32.

You, Homer, and Pong approach the tangled growth of vines and bushes and enter a corridor of the main palace. Fierce-looking creatures are carved into the huge pillars. They have screaming green eyes and red faces. The pillars are wound with carvings of snakes.

A real live snake is wound around one of them.

Homer snugs up to you and whispers, "I don't feel good about this. Too many ghosts of the past. Maybe the old Rama kings are here. Maybe their spirit animals, the elephants, are still here."

"So, what do you think we should do?" you ask.

"I'm too scared. I don't know," Homer admits.

If you decide to 23 skiddoo * * *out of the palace, turn to page 51.*

If you tell Homer to stop worrying, turn to page 44.

(*To scram, to bolt, to leave in a hurry)

34

"You know, Homer old boy, you might just be right. To trust is good—but sometimes, asking questions first is better." You reach down and scratch Homer on the head.

"No time to waste! Let's make tracks," he says.

Wham! You smack right into a huge tree trunk. Wait a minute. It isn't a tree trunk! It's an elephant leg.

The elephant doesn't move. You freeze right where you are. Maybe the elephant didn't notice? Then its trunk swings back and forth in a slow arc. It touches your head. It feels like a pat on the head. Could it be friendly?

Go on to the next page.

The elephant moves its huge head down to look at you eye to eye. Its huge brown eyes look warm and friendly. You know that there is no anger or meanness here.

"Talk to him, Homer. You can speak in all tongues."

Turn to page 37.

"I can speak your language," the elephant says. As he speaks, three other elephants move in a circle around you. You are amazed at how silent they can be.

"We need help," the first elephant says. "Maybe you can come to our aid."

"What is the problem?" you ask. Homer is listening very carefully.

"Illness has fallen on our herd. The young ones are sick and we fear they will die. Maybe you can bring us medicine?"

If you and Homer get in the Socko Speeder and return to home to get medicine, turn to page 57.

If you and Homer decide to visit the sick elephants first, turn to page 66.

"Let me go!" you yell. But the knights just laugh at you. Which one of these knights has the creepy voice?

You look down into the helmet of the knight closest to you.

It's empty! A shiver runs down your arms and legs. Are these robots? Or ghosts?

You look around for Homer, but he is gone. You are alone.

"Don't be afraid. I mean no harm. Come in, come in," the voice says.

If you decide to cut the strange spiderweb holding you captive and escape, turn to page 40.

If you pull the head off the suit of armor to see what's inside, turn to page 42.

You decide to cut the spiderweb. You pull out your pocket knife and open it. Or try to.

"Yuck!" you exclaim. Your knife is all stuck with old cheese and pepperoni from the cold pizza you took on a hike last week.

The empty armor clanks onward into the darkness of the main hall. Rats scurry, bats flap, and snakes slither. This is getting scarier by the second.

One last chance! You remember the chant, the old secret chant handed down to you by a fifth grader.

ANCHOVIES, ICE CREAM, PEANUT BUTTER, FLUFF, GET ME OUT OF HERE, I'VE HAD ENOUGH!

Go on to the next page.

A bright orange flash lights the darkness. The empty armor falls to the stone floor with a clang. The web melts. The voice turns into a whiny kid's voice.

"Ah, don't go! I need a friend. Please don't go!"

But you don't wait to see who it is. You're gone-zo out of there!

The End – or is it?

You lift the head off the knight closest to you. Homer screams with terror. Immediately, all four knights fall to the ground, like a bunch of useless tin cans. You and Homer look at each other and shrug. You step free from the spiderweb.

"I wonder where those ghost knights meant to take us?" you say. You brush some of the spiderweb off Homer's coat.

"I don't know. This place feels funny to me," Homer replies.

"We can handle it," you say. "Follow me. At any rate, we have to find our way out of here."

Slowly you creep through the giant manor house. The hallway with its three-story-high ceiling is chilly and drafty. You can barely see the walls, which are hung with large portraits of former owners of the Hall.

Turn to page 20.

"Buck up, Homer old boy. This is adventure."

You follow Pong toward the other two kids next to the huge pillar. The pillar is shaped like a giant, angry bird-like figure. It has beady eyes, a long beak, and beautiful feathers of gold, green, and crimson.

"This is Garuda, the semi-divine bird creature that all of us in Thailand honor, respect, *and* fear," Pong says. "The real Garuda is said to have wings a mile long! Don't be frightened. He will protect you."

"Protect us from what?" you ask, beginning to think being here at the palace is not such a good idea.

"Protect you from your fears, from the past, and from evil in the future," Pong says.

Turn to page 47.

The Garuda suddenly leans forward and spreads its wings. Each feather holds a human being!

"What is happening?" you scream to Pong. "What is this all about?"

Pong and Ding and Song all kneel as if in prayer.

"It is about destiny. You and Homer have been sent to us to help all children in the world. The Garuda welcomes you. The people in his feathers are here to help you with your journey and task. It is a huge honor."

Turn to page 48.

"What can I do?" you ask, almost pleading. Maybe this is a dream. Or a trick? Who knows? Homer is hiding.

"You can help all the world's children by teaching them to read. You are a great soul, a great spirit. All you need to do now is to accept your role in life. You are a leader."

From that day forth, you dedicate your life to the kids of the world, whether rich or poor. You teach them to read. You help them to realize their own great gifts, and their own special powers.

You are still just a kid, but what a kid!

The End

"Latin?" you say. "Where did you learn Latin?"

"Internet." He shrugs. "You'd be surprised what you can learn there."

"So, what now?" you ask.

"We proceed with caution. *Carpe diem*!" he says. "Seize the day! That's Latin, too. Came from a Roman poet named Horace. A long time ago."

"Boy, you are something else. What do we seize?"

"Opportunity. My sensor says this is not a hostile being. This being needs our help. Follow me."

Homer steps right up to the glowing ball of light and taps it with his paw. You are startled, but the voice gives a throaty chuckle.

Turn to page 60.

"I'm out of here!" you yell.

Homer is way ahead of you, running back up the trail. His tail is between his legs, a sure sign that he is scared.

Once in the jungle, the trail disappears. You hear Pong and his siblings behind you.

"Come back, come back!" they yell. "We need you. Don't leave us!"

Turn to page 53.

A giant bird flies overhead. Is it the Garuda?

The bird continues to circle, its giant wings filling the sky. It *is* the Garuda. The Garuda is a magical bird that is loved and feared. His wings are a mile long. He is a protector. Slowly you and Homer turn around and return to the palace with Pong, Ding, and Song.

The palace and the temple with the giant golden Buddha sitting in it are both free from the bushes and trees growing through them. Only blooming flowers remain, just outside.

"You see, this is our home now. We escaped an evil couple who tried to makes us thieves in Bangkok. Bangkok is a city far from here on the Chao Phraya river. We lived on a houseboat on the river."

"How did you get here?" you ask. You are strangely no longer afraid. The Garuda is back in his place at the pillar.

Turn to page 54.

"One night, Song saw the Garuda overhead. She decided it was a sign. It was time to escape. We followed the Garuda on foot, traveling at night. He led us here, to this wonderful place in the jungle. It is magical. But we need help. Garuda sent you and Homer to us. We know that!"

"How can I help?" you ask. "I'm still a kid."

"Yes, but you know much more than we do. We need someone to teach us. If we are to make our lives better, we need to learn," Pong answers. You realize Pong is right. So starts a powerful part of your life, a part you will never forget. It is a life of teaching and helping others.

The End

"We'll be back," you tell the elephants.

You and Homer rush through the jungle until you get to the clearing.

The Speeder is gone!

What to do?

"Homer, where is it?" you ask.

"I programmed it for invisibility."

He snaps his paws three times and the Speeder appears, ready to go.

Sometimes Homer is amazing, like right now.

Off you zoom, and in mere seconds you are back home. Homer's vet listens to your amazing story, packs a bag, and joins you to return to Thailand and the elephants.

"We're back!" you shout, climbing out of the Socko Speeder. The lead elephant nods his head in recognition.

Turn to page 58.

"We knew you would return. You are a person who keeps a promise. Welcome."

The vet goes to the sick baby elephants, analyzes the illness and treats them. In two days they begin to get well.

The trip was worth it. This was not really a haunted palace after all!

The End

"Hey, cat/voice, who are you?"

"Doubting Thomas are you, then?" the cat says with a purr. "I'm everything you forgot to do, everything that you should have done, and most of the future you want. To trust is good, very good."

"Not much of an answer," you reply.

"As you wish. Not much of a person."

"Okay, okay. You win. What now?" Homer makes low growls, a sure sign that he wants out.

"It's not I that wants, it's you that wants."

"What do you mean?" You are getting tired of this puzzle.

"Ask yourself." The cat/voice vanishes.

Turn to page 70.

"Ah, it's you. I was hoping you'd be brave enough to come," the glowing voice announces.

The face of a Cheshire cat emerges from the glowing light.

"You are the explorer who gets the ghosts out of haunted houses."

"Well, sort of," you reply. Homer makes a jealous face. You ignore him.

"More than a thousand years ago, an older brother locked his younger brother in the basement. His spirit wants to be free. You can do it."

You are stunned.

"Don't worry, the younger brother escaped. It was meant to be a joke."

"So why does his spirit hang around?" you ask.

"You'd have to ask him."

Go on to the next page.

If you take on the job of getting the spirit of the younger brother to give up and go away, turn to page 62.

If you want more info from the voice/cat, turn to page 59. This could be dangerous.

"Okay, I'll do it," you say.

Homer looks scared.

"The basement is down those stairs. Be careful, there might be other spirits there. I don't know..." the Cheshire cat says as he begins to fade away.

Down you go. It is dark, creepy, damp and definitely not fun!

You reach the bottom and click on your flashlight, but the light fails. The door above slams shut.

"Let's go back now," whimpers Homer.

"NO!" you reply, even though you feel a little scared yourself.

Turn to page 65.

So, into the gloom you go. Things scurry by you. A bat flies so close you can hear it. Snakes slither. Slimy pools of gunk block the way.

"Turn back," your brain screams, but a strange power moves you forward.

A door opens along the wall and light pours in.

A voice cries out: "Come up here!"

Up you go reaching a garden filled with summer flowers and fruit-laden trees. In the middle stands a small boy dressed in clothes from many, many years ago.

"Can I go now? Really go? Am I free?" he asks.

"Yes," you reply. "The spell is broken. You are free."

There is a golden flash and the spirit of the young boy disappears.

The curse of Montagoo Hall has ended.

The End

"Let's see the baby elephants right now," Homer says.

You agree, and so the elephants lead you deep into the jungle to their secret hiding place.

Pong is there! What a surprise.

"Hey, where did you guys go?" he asks. One of the baby elephants has his trunk resting on his shoulder, just like kids do with their friends.

Go on to the next page.

You see six more young elephants lying down under several large trees. They don't look well.

You want to help them, but how?

Homer whispers in your ear, "I'll slip back to the Socko Speeder and pick up Dr. Melissa, the vet back home. Be back in a jiff!"

Off he goes.

Now that the jungle, palace, and temple are no longer scary, you turn to Pong.

"So, why are you here, Pong?"

"We are orphans. When we escaped from Bangkok, the elephants took us in. They protect us. Now we want to get other kids here, other orphans, and help them. "

"I'd like to help, too," you say.

"Great," Pong replies.

Go on to the next page.

The two of you start planning how to create a school and dorms and a big kitchen in the old palace. The elephants will help, of course.

"Hey, what about the sick elephants?" you say.

Just then the Socko Skidder appears with Homer and Dr. Melissa, the vet.

This palace and the temple were haunted by good ghosts!

The End

As if in a trance, you lead Homer to a spiral staircase leading to the roof of Montagoo Hall. There in the brilliant sunlight of a summer's day you see YOURSELF.

You were the little child tricked by an older brother. You were the child who lost your way. You are the little child who wants to believe that kindness and goodness are in the hearts of all people.

Now you *do* believe; and you forgive your brother for what he did to you many, many years ago.

The End

ABOUT THE ILLUSTRATOR

Illustrator Keith Newton began his art career in the theater as a set painter. Having talent and a strong desire to paint portraits, he moved to New York and studied fine art at the Art Students League. Keith has won numerous awards in art such as The Grumbacher Gold Medallion and Salmagundi Award for Pastel. He soon began illustrating and was hired by Walt Disney Feature Animation where he worked on such films as *Pocahontas* and *Mulan* as a background artist. Keith also designed color models for sculptures at Disney's Animal Kingdom and has animated commercials for Euro Disney. Today, Keith Newton freelances from his home and teaches entertainment illustration at the College for Creative Studies in Detroit. He is married and has two daughters.

ABOUT THE AUTHOR

R. A. Montgomery has hiked in the Himalayas, climbed mountains in Europe, scuba-dived in Central America, and worked in Africa. He lives in France in the winter, travels frequently to Asia, and calls Vermont home. Montgomery graduated from Williams College and attended graduate school at Yale University and NYU. His interests include macroeconomics, geopolitics, mythology, history, mystery novels, and music. He has two grown sons, a daughter-in-law, and two granddaughters. His wife, Shannon Gilligan, is an author and noted interactive game designer. Montgomery feels that the new generation of people under 15 is the most important asset in our world.

For games, activities, and other fun stuff, or to write to R. A. Montgomery, visit us online at CYOA.com

Watch for these titles coming up in the

CHOOSE YOUR OWN ADVENTURE®

Dragonlarks® series for Beginning Readers

ALWAYS PICKED LAST
YOUR VERY OWN ROBOT GOES CUCKOO-BANANAS
RETURN TO HAUNTED HOUSE
THE OWL TREE
THE LAKE MONSTER MYSTERY
YOUR VERY OWN ROBOT
THE HAUNTED HOUSE
YOUR PURRR-FECT BIRTHDAY
SAND CASTLE
GHOST ISLAND
INDIAN TRAIL
CARAVAN

"Kids this age love the power of choice… these are my child's favorite books!"
— cyoa.com

"This set of books was a big hit with my grandchildren!"
— cyoa.com